W9-ALL-716

Whoo's Too Tired?

Written by Morgan Matthews
Illustrated by Richard Max Kolding

Troll Associates

EAU CLAIRE DISTRICT LIBRARY

102665

Library of Congress Cataloging-in-Publication Data

Matthews, Morgan.
    Whoo's too tired?

    (Fiddlesticks)
    Summary: Edwin Owl has to switch from sleeping all
day to sleeping at night when he goes to work for a
big department store, but the sudden change in his
sleeping habits puts his new job in jeopardy.
    [1. Owls—Fiction.   2. Sleep—Fiction.   3. Department
stores—Fiction.   4. Work—Fiction]   I. Kolding, Richard
Max, ill.   II. Title.   III. Series.
PZ7.M43425Who   1989   [E]   88-1285
ISBN 0-8167-1331-6 (lib. bdg.)
ISBN 0-8167-1332-4 (pbk.)

Copyright © 1989 by Troll Associates, Mahwah, New Jersey
All rights reserved. No part of this book may be used or
reproduced in any manner whatsoever without written
permission from the publisher.
Printed in the United States of America.

10   9   8   7   6   5   4   3   2   1

"*Whooo* boy! Am I ever tired," sighed
Edwin Owl, as he landed in front of his tree
house. He let out a weary yawn and stretched
his wings. The morning sun was just peeking
over the hills.

"I hunted all night, and I didn't find a
thing," Edwin groaned. "Night after night,
it's the same old struggle to make ends meet.
There must be a better way to make a living."

Edwin unlocked his front door and went into the house. "What I need," he said sleepily, "is a good day's rest."

Like all owls, Edwin worked the night shift. He slept when the sun came up and worked when it went down. But lately that was becoming a problem.

The little owl slipped on his pajamas and hopped into bed. He shut his eyes tightly. But did he doze off? Oh no! Tired as he was, Edwin couldn't fall asleep. He tossed and turned and turned and tossed.

The problem was that Edwin had
something on his mind. It was his job.
He fidgeted every time he thought about it.
He wasn't able to make a living at his old
job anymore. And that worried Edwin a lot.
The worrying kept him awake. In fact, poor
Edwin hadn't slept in weeks.

Suddenly, Edwin sat up in bed. He had
made an important decision. "I need a new
job," Edwin said. "And I know where to find
one. A big department store just opened in
town. They have a lot of jobs. I'll go there
this very afternoon and apply for one."
Edwin lay back down. The thought of
getting a new job pleased him very much.
Soon he was sleeping soundly.

When Edwin awoke that afternoon, he put on his best bow tie and his finest shirt. He stood in front of a mirror and carefully preened his feathers. Edwin wanted to look extra nice when he applied for a job. When he was happy with the way he looked, Edwin flew off to the new department store.

At the store he was taken to Mr. Mink's office. Mr. Mink was in charge of the entire store.

"I would like to work here," Edwin said to Mr. Mink. "I'm a good worker. I've worked many years on the night shift."

Mr. Mink smiled. "That's good," he said. "But our store is closed at night. No one works here after dark. Can you work the day shift? We have lots of day jobs."

Edwin rolled his big eyes. He had never worked days before. But he wanted the new job badly.

"I'll work days," Edwin said.

Mr. Mink smiled. "That's great," he said. "We need hard workers. Now, where would you like to work?"

Edwin was puzzled.

"Our store has a lot of departments," Mr. Mink explained. "There is the toy department, the shoe department, and the bedding department, for starters. Which department do you want to work in?"

Edwin was starting to feel tired. He hadn't had enough rest. He yawned and thought about his bed. Bed?

"I'd like to work in the bedding department," answered Edwin.

"Fine," Mr. Mink agreed. "Then it's all settled. Bright and early tomorrow morning, you start work in the bedding department."

That night Edwin went to bed early. He
wanted to be sure he got a good night's sleep.
So, as soon as the sun went down, he hopped
into bed. But his owl eyes opened wide as the
full moon rose.

Edwin pulled the covers up to his chin.
A shiver ran down his spine. What a strange
feeling! He wasn't used to sleeping nights.

"I've got to get some sleep," Edwin said as he flopped on his side. "I don't want to be tired at work tomorrow."

Edwin pulled the covers over his head. But that didn't help. He turned over. He put his head under the pillow. He put his feet on the pillow and his head under the blankets. Nothing helped! Edwin could not fall asleep. He didn't sleep a wink all night!

EAU CLAIRE DISTRICT LIBRARY

The next morning, Edwin was completely exhausted. He showed up at the bedding department so tired he could barely keep his eyes open.

14

A customer walked up to him. "How
comfortable is that bed?" asked the customer.

"It's very comfortable," Edwin replied, as
he walked over to the bed. He sat on the
mattress. "The mattress is very soft."

"Are you sure it's soft and comfortable?" the customer wanted to know. "Is it easy to fall asleep upon?"

"Falling asleep in this bed is easy," Edwin told the customer. "Just watch." Edwin lay down on the bed. He stretched out on the mattress and shut his eyes. He let out a soft sigh. "*Whooo*, that feels good," he murmured.

"My, that bed does look comfortable,"
said the customer. "I'll take it."

But Edwin didn't answer. He didn't bat
an eye. He didn't move an inch.

"I said I'll buy it!" repeated the customer
a little louder. Edwin still didn't move. "I'll
buy it!" shouted the customer at the top of
her lungs. "I'll buy it! I want it!"

Mr. Mink ran over to the customer. "What is going on here?" he asked.

"I want to buy that bed," explained the customer. "But your salesman won't sell it to me. He won't even answer me."

Mr. Mink leaned close to Edwin. *Snore! ZZZZZ! Snore!* Edwin was sound asleep. He was sleeping on the job.

"I'll have another salesman take care of you," Mr. Mink told the customer. When she was gone, Mr. Mink shook Edwin. "Wake up, Edwin!" shouted Mr. Mink. "Wake up this instant!"

Snort! Wheeze! Cough! Edwin's eyes snapped open. He saw Mr. Mink standing there glaring at him.

"Sorry, sir," Edwin apologized. "I didn't mean to fall asleep. I couldn't help myself. I didn't sleep a wink last night. I'm used to working nights and sleeping days, not working days and sleeping nights."

Mr. Mink stroked his chin thoughtfully. "I guess it's okay this time," he said. "After all, you *did* sell a bed." Mr. Mink looked at Edwin. Edwin yawned.

"But I don't think the bedding department is right for you," Mr. Mink added.

"I'll work anywhere," offered Edwin, as he jumped to his feet.

"Good," said Mr. Mink. "We need a waiter in the restaurant. You'll be just in time for the lunch-hour rush."

Edwin hurried to the restaurant and
changed into a waiter's uniform. He didn't
want to lose his job. Quickly, he rushed out
to take his first customer's order.

"What would you like to eat, sir?" Edwin asked politely.

The duck looked up from his menu. "I'll start with soup," he said. "And I don't want the soup hot. I want my soup just barely warm. That's the way I like it."

"Yes, sir! Right away, sir," Edwin replied. "Would you like crackers with your barely warm soup, sir?"

The duck smiled in surprise. "Why, yes I would," he replied. "I love soup with crackers."

Edwin rushed off to get the soup and crackers. He picked up his order in the kitchen and scurried back to the table. He put the soup down in front of his customer.

"What else would you like, sir?" Edwin asked.

The duck scratched his head. "I'm not sure yet," he muttered, as he read through the menu. "Wait here until I decide."

Edwin waited as the duck tried to make up his mind. He waited and waited. The waiting soon made him tired. The longer he waited, the more tired he got. His eyelids started to feel heavy. They began to droop. Slowly, his eyes closed. Once they were shut, he fell fast asleep. And did he ever fall! He flopped right into the duck's soup!

Slosh! Snore! Glub! Glub!

"Get the manager!" said the duck, jumping to his feet. "I want the manager!"

Mr. Mink came running over. "What's the problem?" he asked. "Didn't you get what you ordered?"

"I got what I ordered," quacked the angry
duck. "I got soup."

Mr. Mink was puzzled. "Was there a fly
in your soup?" he asked.

"Not a fly!" squawked the duck. "An owl!
There's an owl in my soup!" And he pointed
at his table. Slumped over the table was
Edwin. His face was in the bowl of soup.
Edwin was snoring loudly.

Snore! Glub! Glub! Snore!

"I'll fix that waiter," Mr. Mink told the angry duck.

Suddenly, the duck felt a little sorry for Edwin. "He really wasn't a bad waiter," the duck told Mr. Mink. "In fact, he was the best waiter I ever had. I just got mad when he fell asleep in my soup."

Mr. Mink nodded. "We'll get you a new waiter and some new soup," he said to the duck.

After the duck was taken care of, Edwin was awakened and sent to Mr. Mink's office.

"I don't know what to do with you," Mr. Mink said. "You're a good worker, Edwin. Everyone likes you. But you keep falling asleep."

The little owl nodded. "I know. I can't help it. Are you going to fire me?"

"I'm giving you another chance.
Tomorrow you'll be our new elevator
operator."

"Thank you, sir," Edwin said. And he
yawned again.

Mr. Mink sighed. "Now go home and try
to get a good night's sleep so you won't fall
asleep tomorrow."

"I will," said Edwin.

That night it was the same old thing. Edwin couldn't sleep. When he reported for work, he was very tired. But he tried his best to stay awake at his new job.

"Going up!" Edwin yawned. Up, up, up
went the elevator. Edwin stopped at every
floor.

"Socks, suits, boots, tacks, and hat racks,"
said Edwin when the doors opened.

"Books, coats, floats, ladles, and cradles,"
he called at another floor.

Soon his elevator was empty.

The elevator went slowly back down.
Soft music came from a speaker in the wall.
The ride was relaxing. The music was
relaxing. And Edwin was so very tired.
The elevator came to a stop between floors.
Edwin slumped over and started to snore.

Before long, a crowd of angry customers gathered in front of the closed elevator doors. They wanted to go up. But there was no elevator.

"What is this all about?" Mr. Mink asked Mr. Badger. It was Mr. Badger's job to find out about problems in the store. Whenever anything went wrong, Mr. Badger studied the problem and then reported to Mr. Mink.

"The elevator is stuck," answered Mr. Badger. "It won't come down."

"Did you call the elevator operator on the intercom?" asked Mr. Mink.

Mr. Badger nodded. "I think the intercom is broken. The operator doesn't answer. And the intercom is making a funny noise. Listen!" Mr. Badger pressed the intercom button.

Snore! ZZZZZZ! Snore!

Mr. Mink recognized the noise. "That's not a broken intercom!" he shouted. "That's a sleeping owl."

Mr. Mink leaned close to the intercom. "Wake up, Edwin!" he called at the top of his lungs. "Wake up right now!"

Edwin jumped! "Oh, no," he groaned as he started down in the elevator. "I did it again."

When Edwin opened the elevator doors, Mr. Mink was waiting for him. Edwin stepped out. A new elevator operator stepped in.

"You didn't sleep last night, did you?" Mr. Mink asked Edwin.

"Working days isn't easy for an owl," Edwin answered meekly.

"Lucky for you those shoppers were so
tired of waiting, they bought more items on
the first floor than ever before," said Mr.
Mink. "Because of that, I'm giving you one
last chance."

Edwin grinned weakly.

"I'm putting you where there are no
customers to worry about," said Mr. Mink.
"It's the gift-wrap department in the
basement. All you have to do is wrap boxes."

"I can do that," Edwin said.

"The question is—can you stay awake?"
said Mr. Mink.

"I hope so," mumbled Edwin.

In the gift-wrap department Edwin wrapped boxes in colorful paper. He tied them up with pretty ribbons and stuck on fancy bows. He wrapped small boxes, big boxes, and giant-sized boxes. He really did a fine job.

And he tried hard not to doze off. "I can't sleep. I've got to stay awake," Edwin said to himself. "I'm working the day shift now."

But it was hopeless. Edwin could not keep
his eyes open. First one eye closed, then the
other one. He lay back on the boxes and
began to snore.

A short time later, Mr. Mink came in to check on him. He found the little owl sound asleep.

"Wake up, Edwin!" yelled Mr. Mink. "Get up and come to my office."

Edwin shook his head and opened his eyes.
He sadly followed his boss into the office.

"I like you, Edwin," said Mr. Mink.
"I want you to work here. But you just can't
stay awake during the day."

Edwin nodded. He knew what Mr. Mink
was going to say next.

Just then, Mr. Badger burst through the
door. "I'm sorry to interrupt," said Mr.
Badger, "but I have an important report to
make."

"What is it?" asked Mr. Mink.

Mr. Badger explained. "Last night after the store closed, there was an accident. The washing machines in the laundry department sprung leaks. Water squirted everywhere."

"How terrible," said Edwin.

"The water got into the soap boxes," continued Mr. Badger. "The soap made bubbles. That's why there were bubbles all over the third floor this morning."

"If only someone had been here to shut off the water, that wouldn't have happened," said Mr. Mink.

Mr. Badger agreed. "But no one works in the store at night."

Mr. Mink thought for a minute.

Then he looked at Edwin. "I think we need to make a new job," said Mr. Mink. "What this store needs is a night watchman."

"It's not easy to find someone to work
nights," said Mr. Badger. "It's very hard to
stay awake all night."

"It's not hard if you sleep all day," said
Edwin.

Mr. Mink winked at Edwin. "Would you
like to be our new night watchman?" he
asked.

"Yes, sir!" said Edwin happily.

"Then go home and sleep the rest of the
day," ordered Mr. Mink. "You start work
tonight."

Edwin rushed right home. He jumped into bed and fell fast asleep. He slept until the sun went down. That night he wasn't a bit tired when he went to work at his new job.

"This is the kind of job I like," Edwin said, as he flew through the empty store.

EAU CLAIRE DISTRICT LIBRARY

And that is how Edwin Owl became the best night watchman the store ever had. And not once did he ever fall asleep on the job!